I Know An Old Laddie....

JEAN LITTLE

Illustrated by ROSE COWLES

VIKING

For my friend Emily Bristowe,
and in memory of our friends
Barney, Abigail and Tiggy
    J.L.

Thanks to Georgia for her days
and to Jeremy for his evenings.
Without your sacrifices
I would never get anything done.
    love Rose (mom)

VIKING
Published by the Penguin Group
Penguin Books Canada Ltd, 10 Alcorn Avenue, Toronto, Ontario, Canada M4V 3B2
Penguin Books Ltd, 27 Wrights Lane, London W8 5TZ, England
Penguin Putnam Inc., 375 Hudson Street, New York, New York 10014, U.S.A.
Penguin Books Australia Ltd, Ringwood, Victoria, Australia
Penguin Books (NZ) Ltd, cnr Rosedale and Airborne Roads, Albany, Auckland 1310, New Zealand

Penguin Books Ltd, Registered Offices: Harmondsworth, Middlesex, England

First published 1999

10 9 8 7 6 5 4 3 2 1
Text Copyright © Jean Little, 1999
Illustrations Copyright © Rose Cowles, 1999

Printed and bound in Hong Kong, China by
Book Art Inc.,Toronto

Canadian Cataloguing in Publication Data

Little, Jean, 1932-
   I know an old laddie—

ISBN 0-670-88085-X

1. Children's poetry, Canadian (English).* I. Cowles, Rose, 1967-
II. Title.

PS8523.I77I3 1999   jC811'.54   C99-930619-7
PZ8.3.L638Ik 1999

Visit Penguin Canada's web site at **www.penguin.ca**

I know an old laddie who swallowed a flea
For no good reason that I could see.
"You'll die," said I.
"*Not me*," said he.

I know an old laddie who swallowed a worm,
A slithery, slippery squirm of a worm,
But he swallowed the worm to catch the flea.
"You'll die," said I.
"*Not me,*" said he.

I know an old laddie who swallowed a rat.
A fat, furry rat fetched in by his cat.
He swallowed the rat to catch the worm,
A slithery, slippery squirm of a worm.
"You'll die," said I.
"Not me," said he.

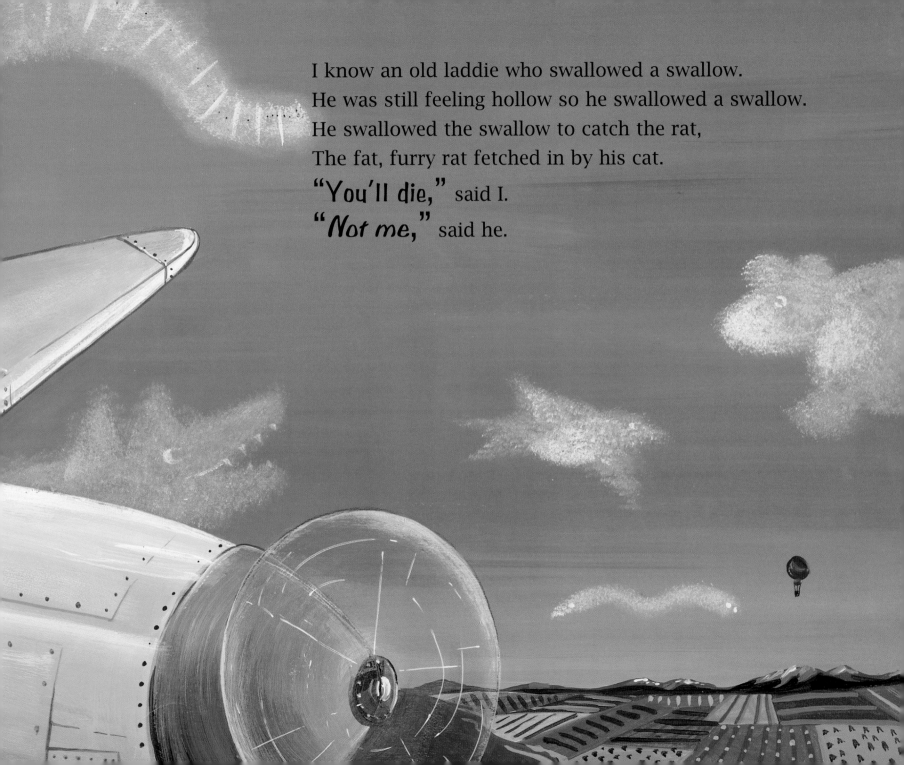

I know an old laddie who swallowed a swallow.
He was still feeling hollow so he swallowed a swallow.
He swallowed the swallow to catch the rat,
The fat, furry rat fetched in by his cat.
"You'll die," said I.
"Not me," said he.

I know an old laddie who swallowed a piranha.
He sat in his sauna and ate a piranha.
He ate the piranha to catch the swallow.
He was still feeling hollow so he swallowed the swallow.
"You'll die," said I.
"Not me," said he.

I know an old laddie who swallowed an eel.
He lengthened his meal with a metre of eel.
He swallowed the eel to catch the piranha.
He sat in his sauna and ate a piranha.
"You'll die," said I.
"Not me," said he.

I know an old laddie who swallowed a puffin.
With a blueberry muffin, he swallowed a puffin.
He swallowed the puffin to catch the eel.
He lengthened his meal with a metre of eel.

"You'll die," said I.
"Not me," said he.

I know an old laddie who swallowed a skunk.
Phew! How he stunk when he swallowed that skunk.
He swallowed that skunk to catch the puffin.
With a blueberry muffin, he swallowed the puffin.
"You'll die," said I.
"*Not me,*" said he.

I know an old laddie who swallowed a possum.
A possum named Blossom. Wasn't that awesome?
He swallowed the possum to catch the skunk,
Phew! How he stunk when he swallowed that skunk.

"You'll die," said I.
"Not me," said he.

I know an old laddie who swallowed a stork.
With a stainless steel fork, he stuffed in a stork.
He swallowed the stork to catch the possum,
A possum named Blossom. Wasn't that awesome?

"You'll die," said I.

"Not me," said he.

I know an old laddie who swallowed a wapiti.
Hippity-hoppity, down went a wapiti.
He swallowed the wapiti to catch the stork.
With a stainless steel fork, he stuffed in a stork.

"You'll die," said I.
"Not me," said he.

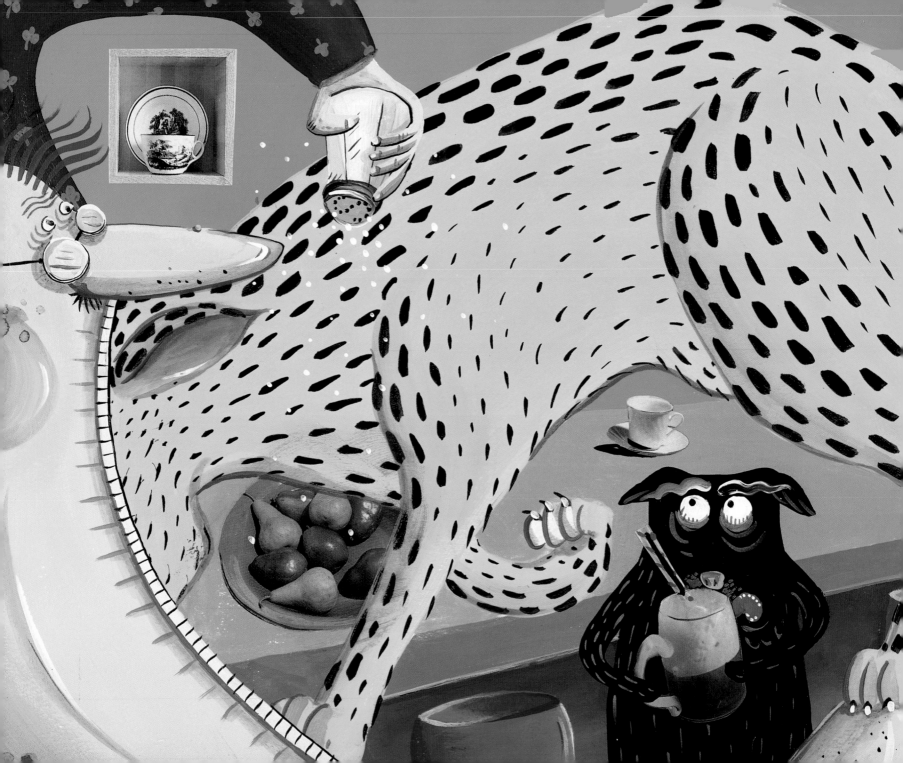

I know an old laddie who swallowed a leopard.
He salted and peppered and swallowed a leopard.
He swallowed the leopard to catch the wapiti.
Hippity-hoppity, down went a wapiti.

"You'll die," said I.

"Not me," said he.

I know an old laddie who swallowed a bear.
Teeth, eyeballs and hair, he bolted that bear.
He bolted the bear to catch the leopard.
He salted and peppered and swallowed a leopard.

"You'll die," said I.

"Not me," said he.

I know an old laddie who swallowed a moose.

His dentures flew loose when he swallowed that moose.

He swallowed the moose to catch the bear.

Teeth, eyeballs and hair, he bolted that bear.

"You'll die," said I.

"Not me," said he.

I know an old laddie who swallowed a giraffe.
It's a bite-and-a-half when you swallow a giraffe
And you can't stop to laugh.
He swallowed the giraffe to catch the moose.
His dentures flew loose when he swallowed that moose.
He swallowed the moose to catch the bear.
Teeth, eyeballs and hair, he bolted that bear.
He bolted the bear to catch the leopard.
He salted and peppered and swallowed a leopard.
He swallowed the leopard to catch the wapiti.
Hippity-hoppity, down went a wapiti.
He swallowed the wapiti to catch the stork.
With a stainless steel fork, he stuffed in a stork.
He swallowed the stork to catch the possum.
The possum named Blossom. Wasn't that awesome?
He swallowed the possum to catch the skunk.
Phew! How he stunk when he swallowed that skunk!
He swallowed the skunk to catch the puffin.
With a blueberry muffin, he swallowed the puffin.
He swallowed the puffin to catch the eel.
He lengthened his meal with a metre of eel.
He swallowed the eel to catch the piranha.
He sat in his sauna and ate a piranha.
He ate the piranha to catch the swallow.
He was still feeling hollow so he swallowed a swallow.
He swallowed the swallow to catch the rat,
A fat, furry rat fetched in by his cat.
He swallowed the rat to catch the worm.
A slithery, slippery squirm of a worm.
He swallowed the worm to catch the flea.

"You'll die," said I.

"*Not me,*" said he.

I know an old laddie who swallowed a squid.

"You'll die," said I.

and

die

he

did!